For Holly and Tes -
the giggliest twins in the world

Text and Illustrations copyright M.P. Robertson 2002, 2014

The right of M.P. Robertson to be identified as the author and illustrator
of this Work has been asserted by him in accordance with the Copyright,
Designs and Patent Act, 1988.

First published in Great Britain in 2002.

This early reader edition first published in Great Britain and in the USA in
2014 by Frances Lincoln Children's Books, 74-77 White Lion Street,
London N1 9PF

www.franceslincoln.com

A CIP catalogue record for this book is available from the British Library.

978-1-84780-549-2

Printed in China

1 3 5 7 9 8 6 4 2

**M.P. ROBERTSON** studied illustration at Kingston University. He is an internationally acclaimed author and illustrator of children's books. His many books for Frances Lincoln include *The Great Dragon Rescue*, *The Egg*, *The Dragon Snatcher*, *Frank 'n' Stan*, *Food Chain*, *Hieronymus Betts and His Unusual Pets* and *Ice Trap!*, written by Meredith Hooper. He lives with his family in Wiltshire. When he isn't writing and illustrating, he enjoys visiting schools to share his love of drawing and stories. To find out more about Mark's books or to book a visit, please go to **www.mprobertson.com**

# BiG
# Foot

## M.P. Robertson

**F**

FRANCES LINCOLN
CHILDREN'S BOOKS

There is a creature lurking in the deep dark woods.

At night he sings his sad song to an ice cold moon.

One fat moon night I heard his song.

I opened my window and played a tune to the trees.
There came a sad reply.

He was very lonely. He needed a friend!

I climbed out into the crisp cold. He had left a trail of footprints. He had very big feet – even bigger than my dad's.

I will call him 'Big Foot', I decided. I followed his trail as it wove deeper and deeper into the dark woods.

Snow began to fall silently. It laid a white blanket
over the trail. I would never find Big Foot now.
I turned towards home, but each tree looked the
same as the last.

The forest had swallowed me up. I sat down and
shivered beneath the ice cold moon.

I took out my flute and played a warming tune.
Then suddenly something stirred. Something big . . .
something hairy! He was as tall as a tree but with
gentle eyes.
It was Big Foot.

"I am lost," I sobbed. "Can you show me the
way home?"
He brushed an icicle tear away from my
cheek, then lifted me onto his broad shoulders.
And together we bounded through the trees.

At the edge of the forest we came to a slope.
It was too steep to walk down.

Big Foot carried me in his lap and we slid together
down the slippery slope.

At the bottom was a frozen lake. It was too slippery to walk across, so we used icicles as skates.

Big Foot was very graceful for one so hairy.

When we reached the other side of the lake, I challenged Big Foot to a snowball fight.

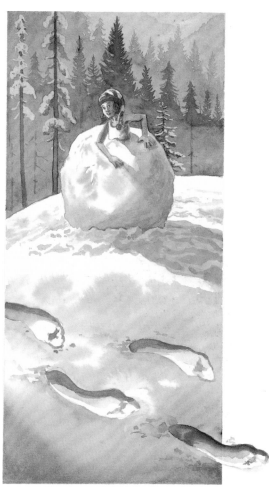

I think he won!

"We should build a snowman," I said.
Big Foot scraped up a mountain of snow and began
to sculpt. But he didn't make a snowman – he made a
snow Big Foot.

When it was finished, Big Foot looked at it sadly, as
though he wished it were real. He wanted another
Big Foot – someone to be his friend.
I brushed an icicle tear from his cheek and kissed
his hairy face. "I know I'm not a Big Foot," I said, "but
I will be your friend."

I suddenly felt very tired. Big Foot rested me on his
back. As we lolloped through the trees I drifted into
warm sleep.

In the morning, Big Foot had gone.

That evening I played my flute to the trees, but there was no reply.

Every evening I did the same, but Big Foot never answered. Had he been just a winter dream?

Then one fat moon night as I played a tune to the trees, I heard his song at last.

He no longer sounded sad, and as I played, his song
was joined by another. Big Foot had found a friend.

# Collect the TIME TO READ books:

978-1-84780-476-1

978-1-84780-475-4

978-1-84780-477-8

978-1-84780-478-5

978-1-84780-543-0

978-1-84780-544-7

978-1-84780-542-3

978-1-84780-545-4

978-1-84780-549-2

978-1-84780-551-5

978-1-84780-552-2

978-1-84780-550-8

Frances Lincoln titles are available from all good bookshops.
You can also buy books and find out more about your favourite titles,
authors and illustrators on our website: www.franceslincoln.com